LOVE LETTERS

**Written & Un-Edited
by Darick Spears**

LOVE LETTERS
ISBN: 978-1-954133-02-0

DDS MEDIAWORKS LLC./21ST CENTURY SHAKESPEARS PUBLISHING

WWW.DARICKBOOKS.COM

GET YOUR BOOK WRITTEN & PUBLISHED TODAY BY

DARICK SPEARS

EMAIL: DARICK@DDSMEDIAWORKS.COM

CALL 414-988-4946

WHY?

WHY AM I ATTRACTED TO YOU?
IS IT BECAUSE OF YOUR ATTRIBUTES?
OR IS IT YOUR ATTITUDE?
WHY DO I LAUGH AT YOUR JOKES?
YOU ARE NOT EVEN FUNNY.
YOU HAVE NO SENSE OF HUMOR,
AND YOU DON'T HAVE ANY MONEY.
YET, I FIND MYSELF DAYDREAMING ABOUT
YOU,
CURIOSITY MIXED WITH TENSION,
THE ATTRACTION IS MYSTERIOUS.
BUT YOU ARE MY WHY,
MY HOW,
MY FUTURE AND MY NOW.
YOU ARE THE REASON WHY I FLOAT OFF
OF GROUND.
AND I DON'T KNOW WHY.

DIMPLES

Your weapon of choice,
a smile.
Diving deeply into a conversation without
words to match.
Your weapon of choice,
a handshake,
an invitation to interpret your mental
landscape.
Your weapon of choice,
a hug.
An intimidating approach,
an entrance into hate or love.
Gods weapon of choice,
your dimples,
a portrait of beauty that could never be
tarnished,
a shatterproof window.

COFFEE

SHE WAS POTENT,
MEMORABLE,
SHE ONLY RECITED DEEP POETIC
CONVERSATIONS.
HER SENSE OF HUMOR WAS DARK,
HER EYES WERE INTIMIDATING.
AS SHE VENTED ABOUT HER
FRUSTRATIONS,
SHE TOLD ME TO CALL HER COFFEE,
INSTEAD I CALLED HER MOCHA,
SHE CORRECTED ME AND TOLD ME
TO CALL HER CULTURE.

THE DIALOGUE PROGRESSED,
PRODUCING HOT WATER CORNBREAD
AND OKRA.
FOOD FOR THOUGHT TURNED INTO
SWEET RED WINE.
TWO MATES WRESTLING WITH A
SNAKE IN THE GARDEN,
THEN INTO THE CAVE OF TREASURES
TO BRING THE CONVERSATION CLOSER.
I WILL NEVER FORGET THAT SIP OF
COFFEE,
THAT DAY I TASTED CULTURE.

TOUGH LOVE

I HONESTLY THOUGHT THAT WE WOULD MAKE IT,
WE HAD PLANS FOR THE FUTURE.
I INVESTED SO MUCH TIME AND EFFORT,
AND ONLY GOT HURT IN RETURN.
TOUGH LOVE.
WE WOULD FIGHT AND MAKE UP,
KISS AND THEN BREAK UP.
TOUGH LOVE.
YOUR TOUCH PUT ME ON ANOTHER PLANET,
BUT YOUR ATTITUDE BROUGHT ME BACK TO EARTH.
YOU TAUGHT ME THAT I HAD NO WORTH,
IT TOOK MANY YEARS FOR ME TO UNLEARN THAT.
TOUGH LOVE.
YOU LET HIM PUT HIS FINGERS IN MY PARADISE,
I LET HER LAY ON YOUR ALTAR.
WE BOTH SINNED,
WE BOTH COULD NOT FORGIVE.
TOUGH LOVE.

I WAS THE ROMEO TO YOUR JULIET,
OUR FAMILIES BOTH DISAPPROVED.
WE FOUGHT TO BE WITH EACH OTHER,
ONLY TO PULL APART.
WE BROKE EACH OTHER'S HEART.
TOUGH LOVE.
YOU GAVE HIM MY PARADISE,
AND THEN YOU TOSSED ME INTO HELLS
FLAMES.
THEN I GAVE YOUR COUSIN MY ALTAR,
THAT WAS INDIRECT FAIR EXCHANGE.
DO I EVER CROSS YOU MIND?
DO I EVER HUNT YOU IN YOUR DREAMS?
SOMETIMES I WISH I COULD HUG YOU ONE
MORE TIME,
THAT TOUGH LOVE GAVE ME A STING.

IMMATURE

I WAS TOO YOUNG TO EMBRACE
YOUR ENERGY,
I MOVED TOO QUICK TO CATCH YOUR
VIBE.
WE WERE ON TWO SEPARATE
TRAIN TRACKS,
TWO DIFFERENT FRAMES OF MIND.
YOU WANTED MORE,
BUT I GAVE YOU LESS.
YOU TRIED TO GIVE ME YOUR
HEART,
BUT ALL I TOOK FROM YOU WAS
SEX.
I WAS IMMATURE.

A MINUTE

PLEASE HEAR ME OUT,
HOP IN THE PASSENGER SEAT
AND LET ME STEER YOU OUT.
LET'S READ SOME TEXT,
ALLOW ME TO POUR YOU A
GLASS OF WINE.
ALL I WANT TO DO IS RELAX IN
YOUR CONVERSATION.

FIRM

A MIND FULL OF CURIOSITY CAN CREATE
UNSTABLE THOUGHTS,
BUT I'M SURE ABOUT YOU.
I AM SO SURE -- THAT I WILL STOP
SEARCHING WITHIN THIS GARDEN,
FOR I HAVE ALREADY FOUND MY FRUIT.
I AM FIRM.
I AM CERTAIN.
I AM SATISFIED.
HOW ABOUT YOU?
DO I MAKE SMILE INSIDE AND OUT?
DO I BRING YOUR FEET OFF OF THE
GROUND?

CAN YOU SEE YOURSELF WITH ANYONE
ELSE?
I HAVE TO KNOW IF OUR FEELINGS ARE
MUTUAL,
I NEED YOU TO BE FIRM.
I NEED YOU TO BE HONEST.
I NEED YOU TO THINK BEYOND THE MOMENT.
EMOTION MAY ONLY LAST A FEW SECONDS,
AFTER TASTING FROM IT'S CUP YOUR
HEART CAN CHANGE DIRECTION.
BUT I AM SURE YOU ARE THE ONE FOR ME,
BUT I WANT TO BE SURE THAT YOU ARE
SURE,
BE HONEST.

Yes___   BE FIRM.   No ___

FANTASIEZ

BATHTUBS AND BUBBLES,
OILS, CANDLES, AND LOTION.
ALL SLOW DANCING WITH AN
ATMOSPHERE FULL OF EMOTION.
THE INCENSE AND WINE,
THE EYE TO EYE CONTRACTS SIGNED
ON THE DOTTED LINES.
THAT STIFF PIECE OF WOOD READY
TO MEET THE JUICE BOX,
CALM WHISPERS, DEEP BREATHS
INHALED AND THEN EXHALED.
PASSION AND FURY,

BITING AND SUCKING,
LIGHTS, CAMERAS AND ACTION,
A SPECTACULAR MOVIE.
AFTER THE WRESTLING SESSION,
COMES THE CONVERSATION THAT IS
INTELLECTUAL.
WHEN WE BOTH EXIT THE
PREMISES THEN WE ARE BACK TO
BEING PROFESSIONALS.
NO MORE PRESSURE FROM OUR
HANDS AND FEET,
WEIGHTS LIFTED OFF,
PURE FANTASIEZ.

LUST

TERRIFIED AND TRAPPED IN YOUR EYES,

YOU KNEW THAT YOU WERE TURNING ME ON.

THE SEDUCTION BEGAN IN YOUR SMILE,

YOUR WALK TOOK ON THE FORM OF A DANCE,

WHILE YOUR MOUTH SPEWED OUT POETIC

LIES.

I WAS FULLY SEDUCED.

WITH THAT BLACK SEE THROUGH JUMP SUIT,

MY HEART WAS BEATING RAPIDLY TO THE

JIGGLE OF THAT RUMP TOO.

LUST.

IT'S YOU THAT I DIDN'T TRUST,

THE DARKNESS HAD TAKEN OVER YOUR

HEART.

NOW YOU WERE ON A MISSION TO PLAY ME

LIKE A HARP.

YOU LET YOUR CLEAVAGE DO THE BARGAINING

WHILE YOU PILED UP THE FEES.

ASKING ME IF I COULD BUY YOU A FEW
THINGS?
PROMISING ME THAT YOU WOULD MODEL
THEM FOR ME.
I WAS TRAPPED IN YOUR LUST.
IT COULD MAKE THE RIGHTEOUS SPEAK
IN WICKED TONGUES.
TRANSFORMING A SMART MIND INTO ONE
THAT'S DUMB,
I WAS A VICTIM OF YOUR MIRAGE,
BUT NEVER AGAIN.
YOU LIED TO ME AND NEVER REPENTED.
BUT IN MY DEFENSE,
I WAS A FOOL IN LUST.

CALM

THE SPICES THAT STEAM OFF YOUR SKIN
LEAVE ME PARALYZED.
MY THROAT IS NOW DRY,
MY FOCUS IS NOREPLY.
TIME MOVES AT A NORMAL PACE,
BUT I AM JUST DECIPHERING IT
DIFFERENT.
MY SPEECH IS NOW SKIPPING,
HOWEVER, I DON'T BELIEVE ANYONE IN
THE WORLD'S LISTENING.
SO I STARE AT YOUR LIPS AS THEY MOVE,
YOUR SKIN AS IT GLISTENS.
PRETENDING THAT WE ARE HOLDING A
DEEP CONVERSATION,
BUT R WE?

I WISH THAT WE WERE.
INSTEAD, I GRAB A PIECE OF PAPER AND
JOT DOWN A FEW CORNY WORDS.

"YOU'RE PERFECT,
YOUR DOPE,
YOU'RE THE OTHER HALF OF MY WORLD.
TOMORROW LET'S MEET HERE AT THE SAME
PLACE -- SAME TIME."

AFTER I FINISHED,
I WAITED FOR THE OPPORTUNITY TO
EMERGE,
AS SHE TURNED TO PICK UP HER JACKET
-- I SLID THE NOTE INTO HER PURSE.
AND THEN I WALKED AWAY CALM.

GEORGINA

I USED TO WRITE YOU ENTICING LETTERS,
BUT THEY ALL FELL ON DEAF EARS.
SADLY,
THERE WAS A CERTAIN DISCONNECT.
YOU MISTOOK MY SILLINESS FOR LIES,
WHEN I WAS BEING TOTALLY HONEST.
I USED TO DAYDREAM ABOUT TAKING YOU SHOPPING,
REACHING INTO MY POCKETS AND HANDING YOU MY
HARD-EARNED MONEY.
BUT TO NO AVAIL.
ALL YOU WOULD DO IS SMILE.
A GRIN FULL OF MYSTERY AND CONFUSION,
I USED TO WRITE YOU POETRY,
BUT MY WORDS NEVER INCITED A RIOT.
YOU REMAINED CALM WITH THAT SAME SMILE,
A TOTAL MISDEMEANOR.
I CAN NEVER UNDERSTAND WHAT I SAW IN
GEORGINA.

FINESSE

You are a piece of
worthlessness,
You really are...
You loved everything about me
except my heart.
And you found a way to crush
that.
How could you say that you
loved me and then kiss him?
You finessed your way into my
world.
And then you deteriorated it
rapidly.

SNAKES FINESSE SO ELOQUENTLY.
AND AM I SURE YOU HAVE BEEN
TOLD THIS.
THE POWER OF THE POWER -U,
THE POWER OF MILKY WAY.
THE POWER OF FINESSE.
YOU ARE A PIECE OF
WORTHLESSNESS,
YOU REALLY ARE...
YOU LOVED EVERYTHING ABOUT ME
EXCEPT MY HEART.
AND YOU FOUND A WAY TO CRUSH
THAT.

LOVE

SUCKS

SOMETIMES....

PAYMENT

LOVE HAS A FINDERS FEE,
AND NOW YOU HAVE A PRICE TO
PAY.
YOU CLAIM TO BE IN LOVE WITH ME,
AND NOW YOU WOULD LIKE TO STAY
THE NIGHT.
BUT I NEED TO KNOW YOUR
PAYMENT PLAN.
ARE YOU COOKING DINNER IN A
THONG?
ARE YOU VOLUNTEERING TO BE MY
SEX SLAVE UNTIL DAWN?
PAYMENT.

I'M NOT BUYING WHATEVER YOU ARE
SELLING,
YOUR WORDS ARE MAKING ME
NAUSEOUS.
I HAVE BEEN HURT BEFORE,
MISLEAD AND TIMES GREW HARDER.
SO, YOUR ACTIONS MUST NOW BE YOUR
BARTER.
SHOW ME WHAT YOU'RE WORKING
WITH,
IT'S REHEARSAL TIME.
AND I PROMISE THAT IF IT'S WORTH IT,
YOUR PAYMENT WILL COME WITH A
FULL REFUND.

LOVE LETTERS

BY DARICK SPEARS

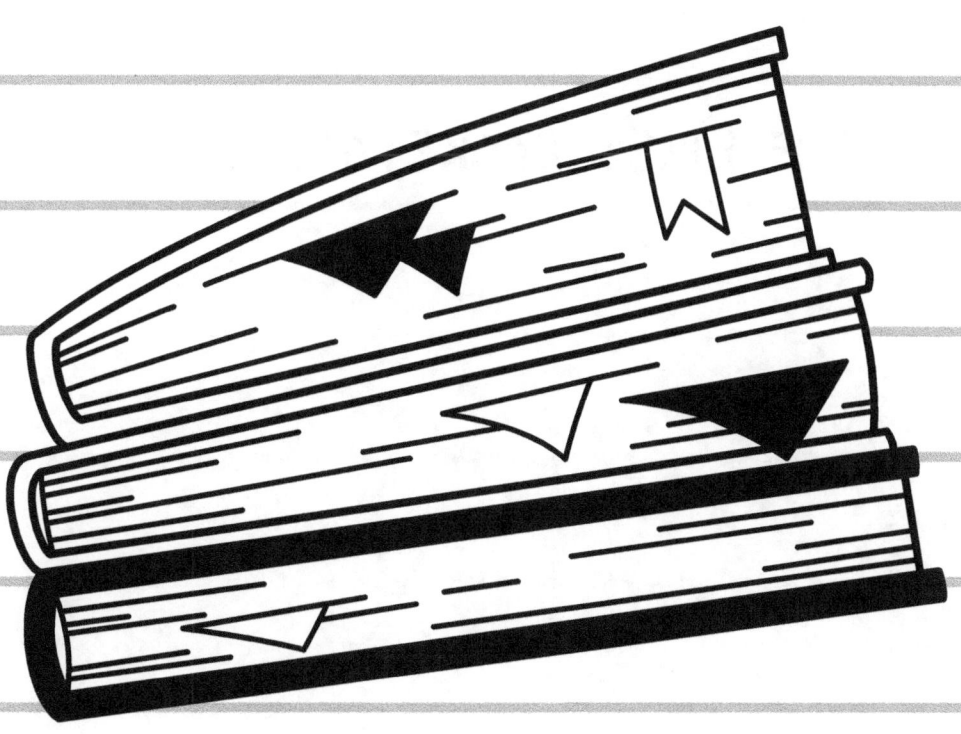

Darick Books

THE FIRST BOOKSTORE OF ITS KIND

www.ingramcontent.com/pod-product-compliance
Lightning Source LLC
Chambersburg PA
CBHW081522050726
47503CB00018B/2953